Dinosaur My Darling

By
Edith Thacher Hurd
Illustrated by
Don Freeman

Harper & Row, Publishers
New York, Hagerstown, San Francisco, London

Library of Congress Cataloging in Publication Data
Hurd, Edith Thacher, date
    Dinosaur, my darling.

    SUMMARY: Joe is surprised to see a live dinosaur when he
digs a hole with his backhoe.
    [1.   Dinosaurs — Fiction]   I.   Freeman, Don.
II.   Title.
PZ7.H956Di   [E]   77-11854
ISBN 0-06-022743-5
ISBN 0-06-022744-3 lib. bdg.

For Don

This is Joe.

This is Joe's backhoe.

Joe lives all alone with his backhoe.
No cats.
No dogs.
No little birds in cages, singing.
Nobody there to care for him,
just Joe and his backhoe.

But Joe is slow with his backhoe.
He has no big PUSHERS or
SHOVERS or
DIGGERS to help him,
just Joe and his little backhoe.

Every day somebody asks Joe to dig
a hole for something:

a little hole for a little house,

a big hole for a big house.

But one day Joe wakes up and thinks,
"Today I have this feeling that
I have to dig a hole just for myself.
I have to dig a hole that's all my own."

So Joe begins to dig.

"What kind of hole today, Joe?"

somebody says.

"I don't know," says Joe.

"But today I have this feeling that

I have to dig a hole just for myself.

I have to dig a hole that's all my own."

Everybody laughs at Joe
because he has to dig a hole of his own
but he doesn't know why.
Then all the people gather round.
They put their eyes to the
little peek-holes in the fence.

Blue eyes.
Green eyes.
Dog eyes.
Cat eyes.
Even little mice eyes.
All the eyes watch through the peek-holes.

"Nobody digs slower than our Joe,"
somebody says.
All the heads nod up and down together.
All the eyes watch Joe.

And everyone is wondering,
is something going into this big hole
or is something coming out of it?

Nobody knows
UNTIL—

"OOO LA LA!" shouts Joe.
"What is that?"

The eyes look.
"OOO LA LA!"
Everyone is shouting.
Everyone is asking,
"What is that?
Joe! Joe!
What is that?"

People climb ladders.
Boys climb flagpoles.
Aviators swoop by in the sky.

Ladies fly by in balloons.
Everyone wants a good look
at the hole that Joe dug
and the THING that is in it.

17

First a head, green and bright,
a huge enormous head,
shiny in the bright sunlight.

Eyes with sparkles.
A nose with holes like tunnels.
And there she is!
The lovely THING!

She blows a puff of steam
and speaks.
"Oh Joe," she says.
"Hello! I have been
asleep for two million
years and I haven't had
a bite to eat."

"OOO LA LA!
Not a bite to eat?" says Joe.
All the eyes look sad.
For two million years, not a bite to eat.
The BIG THING groans and says,

"Bring me lamb chops, thick and juicy.
Bring me applesauce
with yellow custard sauce.
Give me soup made from bananas,
and chocolate drops with pink insides.
Could I please have a little food?
AND HURRY!"

"Yes! Yes! Yes!"
Everyone is shouting.
"Yes!"
Then all the eyes disappear.
Some go to the butcher shop
for one hundred fat lamb chops.
Some go running to the bakery
for cakes and pies:
apple,
raspberry
and Fig Newton pies.

To the candy store for chocolate drops
with pink insides.
They bring back the food
in trucks and cars, and on their bikes.

"Dig me out a little bit,"
the BIG THING says.
"So that I can eat,
more and more and MORE."
"Oh you poor, starving, lovely THING,"
says Joe.

Then Joe and his backhoe begin to dig.
All the people gather round and shout,
"Hurrah! Hurrah! Hurrah for Joe."
At last!
There she is.
A BIG, HUGE, ENORMOUS THING.

Joe feeds her with his backhoe:
tasty pies, ten-layered cakes,
putting bites like mountains
in her mouth.
More and More and MORE.
Until at last,
even such a big thing cannot
tuck in one more chocolate drop.

"Thank you, Joe," she says,
and then she sighs.
"I'm sleepy, Joe.
Bring me a bed.
Bring me a cover.
Bring me a pillow for my head."

Ten men bring ten beds.
Fifteen women bring soft pillows.
Joe brings a little cover
made for him long, long ago
by his old mother.
The lovely THING lies down.
Joe says "Sh-sh-sh," to everyone.
So the whole town is quiet.
No cars honk.
No trucks roar.

Airplanes passing overhead only soar.
People tiptoe on their toes.
Cats do not meow.
Dogs do not bow-wow.
Everyone is quiet and
the sun goes down.

"Oh DINOSAUR MY DARLING,"
Joe says softly to the BIG THING.
"I knew there must be something
waiting in this hole I had to dig."

Just then the BIG THING stirs.
She cannot sleep.
Even on the ten beds,
and the fifteen pillows,
and underneath Joe's little cover,
the BIG THING can only toss and turn.
She cannot sleep.

"I think I'm lonely,"
the BIG THING says.
"Nobody's home.
Nobody's here to care for me.
I haven't got a thing to do,
and I don't want to fall asleep
for another two million years.
What if someone piles dirt all over me again?"

Tears run down the rough green skin,
making lakes and ponds and rivers,
until they almost cover up the ten big beds.
The eyes along the fence close tight.
They don't want to see the
BIG THING crying.

And everyone is thinking,
"Who will take care of this big thing?"
Then all the eyes open wide,
as Joe stands tall on his backhoe
and shouts,
"I will.
I will take care of this poor lonely thing."
Then all the eyes are happy.
All the people say to each other,
"What a brave man is our Joe!"

So Joe runs home to get clean socks,
a toothbrush, and another little cover.
"Oh MY DARLING DINOSAUR!" cries Joe.
Then he stops and whispers.
"You ARE a dinosaur?" says Joe.
"Yes," the BIG THING answers.
"I am your DARLING DINOSAUR,
and you are
MY DARLING JOE."

So the BIG THING and Joe
are never lonely after that.
And now the BIG THING IS ALWAYS BUSY.
And Joe is never slow,
no matter how big a hole
he has to dig.

γ